GIGI

COLETTE

GIGI

Translated by Roger Senhouse

penguin books

PENGUIN BOOKS
Published by the Penguin Group
Penguin Books USA Inc., 375 Hudson Street,
New York, New York 10014, U.S.A.
Penguin Books Ltd, 27 Wrights Lane,
London W8 5TZ, England
Penguin Books Australia Ltd, Ringwood,
Victoria, Australia
Penguin Books Canada Ltd, 10 Alcorn Avenue,
Toronto, Ontario, Canada M4V 3B2
Penguin Books (N.Z.) Ltd, 182–190 Wairau Road,
Auckland 10, New Zealand

Penguin Books Ltd, Registered Offices:
Harmondsworth, Middlesex, England

Published in Penguin Books 1995

Translation copyright Martin Secker & Warburg Ltd, 1953
All rights reserved

Gigi was first published by La Guilde du Livre, Lausanne, 1944. Roger Senhouse's
translation is from the volume *Gigi and the Cat*, which is published in the United
States by Farrar, Straus & Giroux and is available in a Penguin Books edition.

ISBN 0 14 60.0113 3

Printed in the United States of America

Except in the United States of America, this book is sold subject to the condition
that it shall not, by way of trade or otherwise, be lent, re-sold, hired out, or otherwise circulated without the publisher's prior consent in any form of binding or
cover other than that in which it is published and without a similar condition in-
cluding this condition being imposed on the subsequent purchaser.

GIGI

'Don't forget you are going to Aunt Alicia's. Do you hear me, Gilberte? Come here and let me do your curls, Gilberte, do you hear me?'

'Couldn't I go there without having my hair curled, Grandmamma?'

'I don't think so!' said Madame Alvarez, quietly. She took an old pair of curling-irons, with prongs that ended in little round metal knobs, and put them to heat over the blue flame of a spirit-lamp while she prepared the tissue-papers.

'Grandmamma, couldn't you crimp my hair in waves down the side of my head for a change?'

'Out of the question. Ringlets at the very ends—that's as far as a girl of your age can possibly go. Now sit down on the footstool.'

To do so, Gilberte folded up under her the heron-like legs of a girl of fifteen. Below her tartan skirt, she revealed ribbed cotton stockings to just above the knees, unconscious of the perfect oval shape of her knee-caps. Slender calf and high-arched instep—Madame Alvarez never let her eyes run over these fine points without regretting that her granddaughter had not studied dancing professionally. At the moment she was thinking only of the girl's hair. She had corkscrewed the ends and fixed them in tissue-paper, and was now compressing the ash-blonde ringlets between the heated knobs. With patient, soft-fingered skill, she gathered up the full magnificent weight of finely kept hair into sleek ripples which fell to just below Gilberte's shoulders. The girl sat quite still. The smell of the heated tongs, and the whiff of vanilla in the curling-papers, made her feel drowsy. Besides, Gilberte knew that resistance would be useless. She hardly ever tried to elude the authority exercised by her family.

'Is Mamma singing Frasquita today?'

'Yes. And this evening is *Si j'étais Roi*. I have told you before, when you're sitting on a low seat you must keep your knees close to each other, and lean both of them together, either to the right or to the left, for the sake of decorum.'

'But, Grandmamma, I've got on my drawers and my petticoat.'

'Drawers are one thing, decorum is another,' said Madame Alvarez. 'Everything depends on the attitude.'

'Yes. I know. Aunt Alicia has told me often enough,' Gilberte murmured from under her tent of hair.

'I do not require the help of my sister,' said Madame Alvarez testily, 'to instruct you in the elements of propriety. On that subject, thank goodness, I know rather more than she does.'

'Supposing you let me stay here with you today, Grandmamma, couldn't I go and see Aunt Alicia next Sunday?'

'What next!' said Madame Alvarez haughtily. 'Have you any other *purposal* to make to me?'

'Yes, I have,' said Gilberte. 'Have my skirts made a little longer, so I don't have to fold myself up in a Z every time I sit down. . . . You see, Grandmamma, with my skirts too short, I have to keep thinking of my you-know-what.'

'Silence! Aren't you ashamed to call it your you-know-what?'

'I don't mind calling it by any other name, only . . .'

2   Madame Alvarez blew out the spirit-lamp, looked at the re-

flection of her heavy Spanish face in the looking-glass above the mantelpiece, and then laid down the law.

'There is no other name.'

A sceptical look passed across the girl's eyes. Beneath the cockle-shells of fair hair they showed a lovely dark blue, the colour of glistening slate. Gilberte unfolded with a bound.

'But, Grandmamma, all the same, do look! If only my skirts were just that much longer! Or if a small frill could be added!'

'That *would* be nice for your mother, to be seen about with a great gawk looking at least eighteen! In her profession! Where are your brains!'

'In my head,' said Gilberte. 'Since I hardly ever go out with Mamma, what would it matter?'

She pulled down her skirt, which had rucked up towards her slim waist, and asked, 'Can I go in my everyday coat? It's quite good enough.'

'That wouldn't show that it's Sunday! Put on your serge coat and blue sailor-hat. When will you learn what's what?'

When on her feet, Gilberte was as tall as her grandmother. Madame Alvarez had taken the name of a Spanish lover now dead, and accordingly had acquired a creamy complexion, an ample bust, and hair lustrous with brilliantine. She used too white a powder, her heavy cheeks had begun to draw down her lower eyelids a little, and so eventually she took to calling herself Inez. Her unchartered family pursued their fixed orbit around her. Her unmarried daughter Andrée, forsaken by Gilberte's father, now preferred the sober life of a second-lead singer in a State-controlled theatre to the fitful opulence of a life of gallantry. Aunt Alicia—none of her admirers, it seemed, had even mentioned marriage—lived alone, on an income she pretended was modest. The family had a high opinion of Alicia's judgment, and of her jewels.

Madame Alvarez looked her granddaughter up and down, from the felt sailor-hat trimmed with a quill to the ready-made Cavalier shoes.

'Can't you ever manage to keep your legs together? When you stand like that, the Seine could flow between them. You haven't the shadow of a stomach, and yet you somehow contrive to stick it out. And don't forget your gloves, I beg of you.'

Gilberte's every posture was still governed by the unconcern of childish innocence. At times she looked like Robin Hood, at others like a carved angel, or again like a boy in skirts; but she seldom resembled a nearly grown up girl. 'How can you expect to be put into long skirts, when you haven't the sense of a child of eight?' Madame Alvarez asked. And Andrée sighed, 'I find Gilberte so discouraging.' To which Gilberte answered quietly, 'If you didn't find *me* discouraging, then you'd find something else.' For she was sweet and gentle, resigned to a stay-at-home life and seeing few people outside the family. As for her features, no one could yet predict their final mould. A large mouth, which showed beautiful strong white teeth when she laughed, no chin to speak of, and, between high cheekbones, a nose— 'Heavens, where did she get that button?' whispered her mother under her breath. 'If you can't answer that question, my girl, who can?' retorted Madame Alvarez. Whereupon Andrée, who had become prudish too late in life and disgruntled too soon, re-lapsed into silence, automatically stroking her sensitive larynx. 'Gigi is just a bundle of raw material,' Aunt Alicia affirmed. 'It may turn out very well—and, just as easily, all wrong.'

'Grandmamma, there's the bell! I'll open the door on my way out.'

'Grandmamma,' she shouted from the passage, 'it's Uncle Gaston!!'

She came back into the room with a tall, youngish-looking man, her arm linked through his, chattering to him with the childish pomposity of a schoolgirl out of class.

'What a pity it is, Tonton, that I've got to desert you so soon! Grandmamma wishes me to pay a call on Aunt Alicia. Which motor-car are you out in today? Did you come in the new four-seater de Dion-Bouton with the collapsible hood? I hear it can be driven simply with one hand! Goodness, Tonton, those are smart gloves, and no mistake! So you've had a row with Liane, Tonton?'

'Gilberte!' scolded Madame Alvarez. 'What business of yours can that be?'

'But Grandmamma, everybody knows about it. The whole story came out in *Gil Blas*. It began: *A secret bitterness is seeping into the sweet product of the sugar beet* ... At school, all the girls were asking me about it, for of course they know I know you. And I can tell you, Tonton, there's not a soul at school who takes Liane's side! They all agree that she's behaved disgracefully!'

'Gilberte!' repeated Madame Alvarez. 'Say goodbye to Monsieur Lachaille, and run along!'

'Leave her alone, poor child,' Gaston Lachaille sighed. 'She, at any rate, intends no harm. And it's perfectly true that all's over between Liane and me. You're off to Aunt Alicia's, Gigi? Take my motor-car and send it back for me.'

Gilberte gave a little cry, a jump for joy, and hugged Lachaille.

'Thank you, Tonton! Just think of Aunt Alicia's face! The concierge's eyes will be popping from her head!'

Off she went, with the clatter of a young filly not yet shod. 5

'You spoil her, Gaston,' said Madame Alvarez.

But in this she was not altogether speaking the truth. Gaston Lachaille did not know how to 'spoil' anyone—even himself. His luxuries were cut and dried: motor-cars, a dreary mansion on the Parc Monceau, Liane's monthly allowance and birthday jewels, champagne and baccarat at Deauville in the summer, at Monte Carlo in the winter. From time to time he would drop a fat cheque into some charity fund, or finance a new daily paper, or buy a yacht only to resell it almost at once to some Central European monarch: yet from none of this did he get any fun. He would say, as he looked at himself in the glass, 'That's the face of a man who is branded.' Because of his rather long nose and large dark eyes he was regarded on all sides as easy game. His commercial instinct and rich man's caution stood him in good stead, however; no one had succeeded in robbing him of his pearl studs, of his massive gold or silver cigarette-cases encrusted with precious stones, of his dark sable-lined top coat.

From the window he watched his motor-car start up. That year, fashionable automobiles were being built with a slightly higher body and a rather wider top, to accommodate the exaggerated hats affected by Caroline Otero, Liane de Pougy, and other conspicuous figures of 1899: and, in consequence, they would sway gentle at every turn of the wheel.

'Mamita,' said Gaston Lachaille, 'you wouldn't make me a cup of camomile?'

'Two rather than one,' answered Madame Alvarez. 'Sit down, my poor Gaston.'

From the depths of a dilapidated armchair she removed some crumpled illustrated papers, a stocking waiting to be darned, and a box of liquorice allsorts, known as *agents de change*. The jilted man settled down into it luxuriously, while his hostess put out the tray and two cups.

'Why does the camomile they brew at home always smell of faded chrysanthemums?' sighed Gaston.

'It's simply a matter of taking pains. You may not believe it, Gaston, but I often picked my best camomile flowers in Paris, on waste ground, insignificant little flowers you would hardly notice. But they have a taste that is *unesteemable*. My goodness, what beautiful cloth your suit is made of! That deep-woven stripe is as smart as can be. Just the sort of material your father liked! But, I must confess, he would never have carried it with such distinction.'

Never more than once during the course of a conversation did Madame Alvarez evoke the memory of an elder Lachaille, whom she claimed to have known intimately. From her former relationship, real or invented, she drew no advantage other than the close friendship of Gaston Lachaille, and the pleasure to be derived from watching a rich man enjoying the comforts of the poor when he made himself at home in her old armchair. Under their gas-blackened ceiling, these three feminine creatures never asked him for pearls, chinchillas, or solitaire diamonds, and they knew how to converse with tact and due solemnity on scandalous topics traditional and recondite. From the age of twelve, Gigi had known that Madame Otero's string of large black pearls were 'dipped'—that is to say, artificially tinted—while the three strings of her matchlessly graded pearl necklace were worth 'a king's ransom'; that Madame de Pougy's seven rows lacked 'life'; that Eugénie Fougère's famous diamond bolero was quite worthless; and that no self-respecting woman gadded about, like Madame Antokolski, in a coupé upholstered in mauve satin. She had obediently broken her friendship with a 7 school friend, Lydia Poret, after the girl had shown her a solitaire, set as a ring, the gift of Baron Ephraim.

'A solitaire!' Madame Alvarez had exclaimed. 'For a girl of fifteen! Her mother must be mad!'

'But Grandmamma,' pleaded Gigi, 'it's not Lydia's fault if the Baron gave it to her!'

'Silence! I'm not blaming the Baron. The Baron knows what is expected of him. But plain common-sense should have told the mother to put the ring in a safe at the Bank, while waiting.'

'While waiting for what, Grandmamma?'

'To see how things turn out.'

'Why not in her jewel-case?'

'Because one never knows. Especially as the Baron is the sort of man who might change his mind. If, on the other hand, he has declared himself openly, Madame Poret has only to withdraw her daughter from her studies. Until the matter has been properly cleared up, you will oblige me by not walking home with that little Poret. Whoever heard of such a thing!'

'But supposing she marries, Grandmamma?'

'Marries? Marries whom, pray?'

'Why, the Baron!'

Madame Alvarez and her daughter exchanged glances of stupefaction. 'I find the child so discouraging,' Andrée had murmured. 'She comes from another planet.'

'My poor Gaston,' said Madame Alvarez, 'is it really true, then, that you have broken with her? In some ways it may be the best thing for you; but in others I'm sure you must find it most upsetting. Whom can one trust, I ask you!'

Poor Gaston listened while he drank the scalding camomile. The taste of it gave him as much comfort as the sight of the

8 plaster rose on the ceiling, still black from the hanging lamp now

'converted to electricity', and still faithfully retaining its shade —a vast frilly bell of palest green. Half the contents of a work-basket lay strewn over the dining-room table, from which Gilberte had forgotten to remove her copy-book. Above the upright piano hung an enlarged photograph of Gilberte at eight months, as a pendant to a portrait in oils of Andrée, dressed for her part in *Si j'étais Roi*. The perfectly inoffensive untidiness, the ray of spring sunshine coming through the point-lace curtains, the warmth given out by a little stove kept at a low heat— all these homely things were like so many soothing potions to the nerves of a jilted and lonely millionaire.

'Are you positively in torment, my poor Gaston?'

'To be exact, I'm not in torment. I'm just very upset, as you say.'

'I have no wish to appear inquisitive,' said Madame Alvarez, 'but how did it all happen? I've read the papers, of course; but can one believe what they say?'

Lachaille tugged at his small waxed moustache, and ran his fingers over his thick, cropped hair.

'Oh, much the same as on previous occasions. She waited for her birthday present, then off she trotted. And, into the bargain, she must needs go and bury herself in such a wretched little hole in Normandy—so stupid of her! Any fool could have discovered that there were only two rooms at the inn, one occupied by Liane, the other by Sandomir, a skating instructor from the *Palais de Glace*.'

'He's Polaire's tea-time waltzing-partner, isn't he? Oh, women don't know where to draw the line nowadays. And just after her birthday, too! Oh, it's so tactless! What could be more unlady-like!'

Madame Alvarez stirred the tea-spoon round and round in 9

her cup, her little finger in the air. When she lowered her gaze, her lids did not quite cover her protuberant eyeballs, and her resemblance to George Sand became marked.

'I'd given her a rope,' said Gaston Lachaille. 'What you might call a rope—thirty-seven pearls. The middle one as big as the ball of my thumb.'

He held out his white, beautifully manicured thumb, to which Madame Alvarez accorded the admiration due to a middle pearl.

'You certainly know how to do things in style,' she said. 'You come out of it extremely well, Gaston.'

'I came out of it with a pair of horns, certainly.'

Madame Alvarez did not seem to have heard him.

'If I were you, Gaston, I should try to get your own back on her. I should take up with some society lady.'

'That's a nice pill to offer me,' said Lachaille, who was absent-mindedly helping himself to the *agents de change*.

'Yes indeed, I might even say that sometimes the cure may prove worse than the disease,' Madame Alvarez continued, tactfully agreeing with him. 'Out of the frying-pan into the fire.' After which she respected Gaston Lachaille's silence.

The muffled sounds of a piano penetrated through the ceiling. Without a word, the visitor held out his empty cup, and Madame Alvarez refilled it.

'Is the family all right? What news of Aunt Alicia?'

'Oh, my sister, you know, is always the same. She's smart enough to keep herself to herself. She says she would rather live in a splendid past than an ugly present. Her King of Spain, her Milan of Serbia, her Khedive, her rajahs by the half-dozen—or so she would have you believe! She is very considerate to Gigi.
10 She finds her a trifle backward for her age, as indeed she is, and

puts her through her paces. Last week, for instance, she taught her how to eat *homard à l'Américaine* in faultless style.'

'Whatever for?'

'Alicia says it will be extremely useful. The three great stumbling-blocks in a girl's education, she says, are *homard à l'Américaine*, a boiled egg, and asparagus. Shoddy table manners, she says, have broken up many a happy home.'

'That has been known,' said Lachaille dreamily.

'Oh, Alicia is no fool! And it's just what Gigi requires—she is so greedy! If only her brain worked as well as her jaws! But she might well be a child of ten. And what breathtaking scheme have you got for the Battle of Flowers? Are you going to dazzle us again this year?'

'Oh Lord, no!' groaned Gaston. 'I shall take advantage of my misfortune, and save on the red roses this year.'

Madame Alvarez wrung her hands.

'Oh, Gaston, you mustn't do that! If you're not there, the procession will look like a funeral!'

'I don't care what it looks like,' said Gaston gloomily.

'You're never going to leave the prize banner to people like Valérie Cheniaguine? Oh, Gaston, we can't allow that!'

'You will have to. Valérie can very well afford it.'

'Especially since she does it on the cheap. Gaston, do you know where she went for the ten thousand bunches thrown last year? She had three women tying them up for two days and two nights, and the flowers were bought in the market! In the market! Only the four wheels, and the coachman's whip, and the harness trappings bore the hallmark of Lachaume.'

'That's a dodge to remember!' said Lachaille, cheering up. 'Good Lord! I've finished the liquorice!'

The tap-tap of Gilberte's marching footsteps could be heard crossing the outer room.

'Back already!' said Madame Alvarez. 'What's the meaning of this?'

'The meaning,' said the girl, 'is that Aunt Alicia wasn't in good form. But I've been out in Tonton's "tuf-tuf".'

Her lips parted in a bright smile.

'You know, Tonton, all the time I was in your automobile, I put on a martyred expression—like this—as if I was bored to death with every luxury under the sun. I had the time of my life.'

She sent her hat flying across the room, and her hair fell tumbling over her forehead and cheeks. She perched herself on a rather high stool, and tucked her knees up under her chin.

'Well, Tonton? You look as if you were dying of boredom. What about a game of piquet? It's Sunday, and Mamma doesn't come back between the two performances. Who's been eating all my liquorice? Oh, Tonton, you can't get away with that! The least you can do is to send me some more to make up for it.'

'Gilberte, your manners!' scolded Madame Alvarez. 'Your knees! Gaston hasn't the time to bother about your liquorice. Pull down your skirts! Gaston, would you like me to send her to her room?'

Young Lachaille, with one eye on the dirty pack of cards in Gilberte's hand, was longing simultaneously to give way to tears, to confide his sorrows, to go to sleep in the old armchair, and to play piquet.

'Let the child stay! In this room I can relax. It's restful. Gigi, I'll play you for twenty pounds of sugar.'

'Your sugar's not very tempting. I much prefer sweets.'

'It's the same thing. And sugar is better for you than sweets.'

'You only say that because you make it.'

'Gilberte, you forget yourself!'

A smile enlivened the mournful eyes of Gaston Lachaille.

'Let her say what she likes, Mamita. And if I lose, Gigi, what would you like? A pair of silk stockings?'

The corners of Gilberte's big, childish mouth fell.

'Silk stockings make my legs itch. I would rather . . .'

She raised the snub-nosed face of an angel towards the ceiling, put her head on one side, and tossed her curls from one cheek to the other.

'I would rather have an eau-de-nil Persephone corset, with ro-coco roses embroidered on the suspenders. No. I'd rather have a music-case.'

'Are you studying music now?'

'No, but my older friends at school carry their copy-books in music-cases, because it makes them look like students at the Conservatoire.'

'Gilberte, you are making too free!' said Madame Alvarez.

'You shall have your case, and your liquorice. Cut, Gigi.'

The next moment, the heir of Lachaille-Sugar was deep in the game. His prominent nose, large enough to appear false, and his slightly negroid eyes did not in the least intimidate his opponent. With her elbows on the table, her shoulders on a level with her ears, and her blue eyes and red cheeks at their most vivid, she looked like a tipsy page. They both played passionately, almost in silence, exchanging occasional insults under their breath. 'You spindly spider! You sorrel run to seed!' Lachaille muttered. 'You old crow's beak!' the girl countered. The March twilight deepened over the narrow street.

'Please don't think I want you to go, Gaston,' said Madame 13

Alvarez, 'but it's half-past seven. Will you excuse me while I just see about our dinner?'

'Half-past seven!' cried Lachaille, 'and I'm supposed to be dining at Larue with de Dion, Feydeau, and one of the Barthous! This must be the last hand, Gigi.'

'Why one of the Barthous?' asked Gilberte. 'Are there several of them?'

'Two. One handsome and the other less so. The best known is the least handsome.'

'That's not fair,' said Gilberte. 'And Feydeau, who's he?'

Lachaille plopped down his cards in amazement.

'Well, I declare! She doesn't know who Feydeau is! Don't you ever go to a play?'

'Hardly ever, Tonton.'

'Don't you like the theatre?'

'I'm not mad about it. And Grandmamma and Aunt Alicia both say that going to plays prevents one from thinking about the serious side of life. Don't tell Grandmamma I told you.'

She shifted the weight of her hair away from her ears, and let it fall forward again. 'Phew!' she sighed. 'This mane does make me hot!'

'And what do they mean by the serious side of life?'

'Oh, I don't know it all off by heart, Uncle Gaston. And, what's more, they don't always agree about it. Grandmamma says: "Don't read novels, they only depress you. Don't put on powder, it ruins the complexion. Don't wear stays, they spoil the figure. Don't dawdle and gaze at shop windows when you're by yourself. Don't get to know the families of your school friends, especially not the fathers who wait at the gates to fetch their daughters home from school." '

She spoke very rapidly, panting between words like a child who has been running.

'And on top of that Aunt Alicia goes off on another tack! I've reached the age where I can wear stays, and I should take lessons in dancing and deportment, and I should be aware of what's going on, and know the meaning of "carat", and not be taken in by the clothes that actresses wear. "It's quite simple," she tells me. "Of all the dresses you see on the stage, nineteen out of twenty would look ridiculous in the paddock." In fact, my head is fit to split with it all! What shall you be eating at Larue this evening, Tonton?'

'How should I know! *Filets de sole aux moules*, for a change. And of course, saddle of lamb with truffles. Do get on with the game, Gigi! I've got a point of five.'

'That won't get you anywhere. I've got all the cards in the pack. Here, at home, we're having the warmed-up remains of the *cassoulet*. I'm very fond of *cassoulet*.'

'A plain dish of *cassoulet* with bacon rind,' said Inez Alvarez modestly, as she came in. 'Goose was exorbitant this week.'

'I'll have one sent to you from Bon-Abri,' said Gaston.

'Thank you very much, Gaston. Gigi, help Monsieur Lachaille on with his overcoat. Fetch him his hat and stick!'

When Lachaille had gone, rather sulky after a regretful sniff at the warmed up *cassoulet*, Madame Alvarez turned to her granddaughter.

'Will you please inform me, Gilberte, why it was you returned so early from Aunt Alicia's? I didn't ask you in front of Gaston. Family matters must never be discussed in front of a third person, remember that!'

'There's no mystery about it, Grandmamma. Aunt Alicia was wearing her little lace cap to show me she had a headache. She said to me, "I'm not very well." I said to her, "Oh, then I mustn't tire you out. I'll go home again." She said to me, "Sit down and rest for five minutes." "Oh!" I said to her, "I'm not tired. I drove here." "You drove here!" she said to me, raising her hands like this. As you may imagine, I had kept the motor-car waiting a few minutes, to show Aunt Alicia. "Yes," I said to her. "The four-seater de-Dion-Bouton-with-the-collapsible-hood, which Tonton lent me while he was paying a call on us. He has had a rumpus with Liane." "Who do you think you're talking to?" she says to me. "I've not yet got one foot in the grave! I'm still kept informed about public events when they're important. I know that he has had a rumpus with that great lamp-post of a woman. Well, you'd better run along home, and not bother about a poor ill old creature like me." She waved to me from the window as I got into the motor-car.'

Madame Alvarez pursed her lips.

'A poor ill old creature! She has never suffered so much as a cold in her life! I like that! What . . . ?'

'Grandmamma, do you think he'll remember my liquorice and the music-case?'

Madame Alvarez slowly lifted her heavy eyes towards the ceiling.

'Perhaps, my child, perhaps.'

'But, as he lost, he owes them to me, doesn't he?'

'Yes, yes, he owes them to you. Perhaps you'll get them after all. Slip on your pinafore, and set the table. Put away your cards.'

'Yes, Grandmamma. Grandmamma, what did he tell you about Madame Liane? Is it true she hopped it with Sandomir and the rope of pearls?'

'In the first place, one doesn't say "hopped it". In the second, come here and let me tighten your ribbon, so that your curls won't get soaked in the soup. And finally, the sayings and doings of a person who has broken the rules of etiquette are not for your ears. These happen to be Gaston's private affairs.'

'But, Grandmamma, they are no longer private, since everyone's talking about them, and the whole thing came out in *Gil Blas*.'

'Silence! All you need to know is that the conduct of Madame Liane d'Exelmans has been the reverse of sensible. The ham for your mother is between two plates: you will put it in the larder.'

Gilberte was asleep when her mother—Andrée Alvar, in small type on the Opéra-Comique play-bills—returned home. Madame Alvarez, the elder, seated at a game of patience, enquired from force of habit whether she was not too tired. Following polite family custom, Andrée reproached her mother for having waited up, and Madame Alvarez made her ritual reply.

'I shouldn't sleep in peace unless I knew you were in. There is some ham, and a little bowl of warm *cassoulet*. And some stewed prunes. The beer is on the window-sill.'

'The child is in bed?'

'Of course.'

Andée Alvar made a solid meal—pessimists have good appetites. She still looked pretty in theatrical make-up. Without it, the rims of her eyes were pink and her lips colourless. For this reason, Aunt Alicia declared, Andrée never met with the admiration in real life that she gained on the stage.

'Did you sing well, my child?'

'Yes, I sang well. But where does it get me? All the applause goes to Tiphaine, as you may well imagine. Oh dear, oh dear, I really don't think I can bear to go on with this sort of life.'

'It was your own choice. But you would bear it much better,' said Madame Alvarez sententiously, 'if you had someone! It's your loneliness that gets on your nerves, and you take such black views. You're behaving contrary to nature.'

'Oh, Mother, don't start that all over again. I'm tired enough as it is. What news is there?'

'None. Everyone's talking of Gaston's break with Liane.'

'That's certainly the case: even in the green-room at the Opéra-Comique, which can hardly be called up-to-date.'

'It's an event of world-wide interest,' said Madame Alvarez. 'Is there any idea of who's in the running?'

'I should think not! It's far too recent. He is in full mourning, so to speak. Can you believe it, at a quarter to eight he was sitting exactly where you are now, playing a game of piquet with Gigi? He says he has no wish to attend the Battle of Flowers.'

'Not really!'

'Yes. If he doesn't go, it will cause a great deal of talk. I advised him to think twice before taking such a decision.'

'They were saying at the Théâtre that a certain music-hall artiste might stand a chance,' said Andrée. 'The one billed as the Cobra at the Olympia. It seems she does an acrobatic turn, and is brought on in a basket hardly big enough for a fox-terrier, and from this she uncurls like a snake.'

Madame Alvarez protruded her heavy lower lip in contempt.

'What an idea! Gaston Lachaille has not sunk to that level! A music-hall performer! Do him the justice to admit that, as befits a bachelor of his standing, he has always confined himself to the great ladies of the profession.'

'A fine pack of bitches!' murmured Andrée.

'Be more careful how you express yourself, my child. Calling
18 people and things by their names has never done anyone any

good. Gaston's mistresses have all had an air about them. A liaison with a great professional lady is the only suitable way for him to wait for a great marriage, always supposing that some day he does marry. Whatever may happen, we're in the front row when anything fresh turns up. Gaston has such confidence in me! I wish you had seen him asking me for camomile! A boy, a regular boy! Indeed, he is only thirty-three. And all that wealth weighs so heavily on his shoulders.'

Andrée's pink eyelids blinked ironically.

'Pity him, Mother, if you like. I'm not complaining, but all the time we've known Gaston, he has never given you anything except his confidence.'

'He owes us nothing. And thanks to him we've always had sugar for our jams, and, from time to time, for my *curaçao*; and birds from his farm, and odds and ends for the child.'

'If you're satisfied with that!'

Madame Alvarez held high her majestic head.

'Perfectly satisfied. And even if I was not, what difference would it make?'

'In fact, as far as we're concerned, Gaston Lachaille, rich as he is, behaves as if he wasn't rich at all. Supposing we were in real straits! Would he come to our rescue, do you suppose?'

Madame Alvarez placed her hand on her heart.

'I'm convinced that he would,' she said. And after a pause, she added, 'But I would rather not have to ask him.'

Andrée picked up the *Journal* again, in which there was a photograph of Liane the ex-mistress. 'When you take a good look at her, she's not so extraordinary.'

'You're wrong,' retorted Madame Alvarez. 'She is extraordinary. Otherwise she would not be so famous. Success and celebrity are not a matter of luck. You talk like those scatterbrains 19 who say, "Seven rows of pearls would look every bit as well on me as on Madame de Pougy. She certainly cuts a dash—but so could I." Such nonsense makes me laugh. Take what's left of the camomile to bathe your eyes.'

'Thank you, Mother. Did the child go to Aunt Alicia's?'

'She did indeed, and in Gaston's motor-car, what's more! He lent it to her. It can go at forty miles an hour, I believe! She was in the seventh heaven.'

'Poor lamb, I wonder what she'll make of her life. She's quite capable of ending up as a mannequin or a saleswoman. She's so backward. At her age, I—'

There was no indulgence in the glance Madame Alvarez bestowed on her daughter.

'Don't boast too much about what you were doing when you were her age. If I remember rightly, at her age you were snapping your fingers at Monsieur Mennesson and all his flour-mills, though he was perfectly ready to make you your fortune. Instead, you must needs bolt with a wretched music-master.'

Andrée Alvar kissed her mother's lustrous plaits.

'My darling Mother, don't curse me at this hour. I'm so sleepy. Good night, Mother. I've a rehearsal tomorrow at a quarter to one. I'll eat at the tea-shop during the interval; don't bother about me.'

She yawned and walked in the dark through the little room where her daughter was asleep. All she could see of Gilberte in the obscurity was a brush of hair and the Russian braid of her nightdress. She locked herself into the exiguous bathroom and, late though it was, lit the gas under a kettle. Madame Alvarez had instilled into her progeny, among other virtues, a respect for certain rites. One of her maxims was, 'You can, at a pinch, leave the face till the morning, when travelling or pressed for time.

For a woman, attention to the lower parts is the first law of self-respect.'

The last to go to bed, Madame Alvarez was the first to rise, and allowed the daily woman no hand in preparing the breakfast coffee. She slept in the dining-sitting-room, on a divan-bed, and, at the stroke of half-past seven, she opened the door to the papers, the quart of milk, and the daily woman—who was carrying the others. By eight o'clock she had taken out her curling pins, and her beautiful coils were dressed and smooth. At ten minutes to nine Gilberte left for school, clean and tidy, her hair well brushed. At ten o'clock Madame Alvarez was 'thinking about' the midday meal, that is, she got into her mackintosh, slipped her arm through the handle of her shopping net, and set off to market.

On that day, as on all other days, she made sure that her granddaughter would not be late; she placed the coffee-pot and the jug of milk piping hot on the table, and unfolded the newspaper while waiting for her. Gilberte came in fresh as a flower, smelling of lavender-water, with some vestiges of sleep still clinging to her. A cry from Madame Alvarez made her fully wide awake.

'Call your mother, Gigi! Liane d'Exelmans has committed suicide.'

The child replied with a long drawn-out 'Oooh!' and asked, 'Is she dead?'

'Of course not. She knows what she's about.'

'How did she do it, Grandmamma? A revolver?'

Madame Alvarez looked pityingly at her granddaughter.

'The idea! Laudanum, as usual.' *"Doctors Morèze and Pelledoux, who have never left the heart-broken beauty's bedside, cannot* 21 *yet answer for her life, but their diagnosis is reassuring . . ."* My own diagnosis is that if Madame d'Exelmans goes on playing that game, she'll end by ruining her stomach.'

'The last time she killed herself, Grandmamma, was for the sake of Prince Georgevitch, wasn't it?'

'Where are your brains, my darling? It was for Count Berthou de Sauveterre.'

'Oh, so it was. And what will Tonton do now, do you think?'

A dreamy look passed across the huge eyes of Madame Alvarez.

'It's a toss-up, my child. We shall know everything in good time, even if he starts by refusing to give an interview to anybody. You must always start by refusing to give an interview to anybody. Then later you can fill the front page. Tell the concierge, by the way, to get us the evening papers. Have you had enough to eat? Did you have your second cup of milk, and your two pieces of bread and butter? Put on your gloves before you go out. Don't dawdle on the way. I'm going to call your mother. What a story! Andrée, are you asleep? Oh, so you're out of bed! Andrée, Liane has committed suicide!'

'That's a nice change!' muttered Andrée. 'She's only the one idea in her head, that woman, but she sticks to it.'

'You've not taken out your curlers yet, Andrée?'

'And have my hair go limp in the middle of rehearsal? No thank you!'

Madame Alvarez ran her eyes over her daughter, from the spiky tips of her curlers to the felt slippers. 'It's plain that there's no man here for you to bother about, my child! A man in the house soon cures a woman of traipsing about in dressing-gown and slippers. What an excitement, this suicide! Unsuccessful, of course.'

Andrée's pallid lips parted in a contemptuous smile: 'It's getting too boring—the way she takes laudanum as if it was castor oil!'

'Anyhow, who cares about her? It's the Lachaille heir who matters. This is the first time such a thing has happened to him. He's already had, let me see. He's had Gentiane, who stole certain papers; then that foreigner, who tried to force him into marriage; but Liane is his first suicide. In such circumstances, a man so much in the public eye has to be extremely careful about what line he takes.'

'Him! He'll be bursting with pride, you may be sure.'

'And with good reason, too,' said Madame Alvarez. 'We shall be seeing great things before very long. I wonder what Alicia will have to say about the situation.'

'She'll do her best to make a mountain out of a molehill.'

'Alicia is no angel. But I must confess that she is far-sighted. And that without ever leaving her room!'

'She's no need to, since she has the telephone. Mother, won't you have one put in here?'

'It's expensive,' said Madame Alvarez, thoughtfully. 'We only just manage to make both ends meet, as it is. The telephone is of real use only to important businessmen, or to women who have something to hide. Now, if you were to change your mode of life—and I'm only putting it forward as a supposition—and if Gigi were to start on a life of her own, I should be the first to say, "We'll have the telephone put in." But we haven't reached that point yet, unfortunately.'

She allowed herself a single sigh, pulled on her rubber gloves, and coolly set about her household chores. Thanks to her care, the oldest flat was growing old without too many signs of deterioration. She retained, from her past life, the honourable habits of women who have lost their honour, and these she taught to her daughter and her daughter's daughter. Sheets never stayed on the beds longer than ten days, and the char-cum-washerwoman told everyone that the chemises and drawers of the ladies of Madame Alvarez' household were changed more often than she could count, and so were the table napkins. At any moment, at the cry of 'Gigi, take off your shoes!' Gilberte had to remove shoes and stockings, exhibit white feet to the closest inspection, and announce the least suspicion of a corn.

During the week following Madame d'Exelman's suicide, Lachaille's reactions were somewhat incoherent. He engaged the stars of the National Musical Academy to dance at a midnight fête held at his own house, and, wishing to give a supper party at the Pré-Catalan, he arranged for that restaurant to open a fortnight earlier than was their custom. The clowns, Footit et Chocolat, did a turn: Rita del Erido caracoled on horseback between the supper tables, wearing a divided skirt of white lace flounces, a white hat on her black hair with white ostrich feathers frothing round the relentless beauty of her face. Indeed, Paris mistakenly proclaimed, such was her beauty, that Gaston Lachaille was about to hoist her (astride) upon a throne of sugar. Twenty-four hours later, Paris remedied the mistake. For, owing to the false prophecies it had published, *Gil Blas* nearly lost the subsidy it received from Gaston Lachaille. A specialized weekly, *Paris en amour*, provided another red herring, under the headline: '*Young Yankee millionairess makes no secret of weakness for French sugar*'.

Madame Alvarez' ample bust shook with incredulous laughter when she read the daily papers; she had received her information from none other than Gaston Lachaille in person. Twice in ten days, he had found time to drop in for a cup of camomile, to sink into the depths of the now sagging conch-shaped arm-chair, and there forget his business worries and his dislike of be-ing unattached. He even brought Gigi an absurd Russian leather music-case with a silver-gilt clasp, and twenty boxes of liquorice. Madame Alvarez was given a *pâté de foie gras* and six bottles of champagne, and of these bounties Tonton Lachaille partook by inviting himself to dinner. Throughout the meal, Gilberte regaled them rather tipsily with tittle-tattle about her school, and later won Gaston's gold pencil at piquet. He lost with good grace, recovered his spirits, laughed and, pointing to the child, said to Madame Alvarez, 'There's my best pal!' Madame Alvarez' Spanish eyes moved with slow watchfulness from Gigi's reddened cheeks and white teeth to Lachaille, who was pulling her hair by the fistful. 'You little devil, you'd the fourth king up your sleeve all the time!'

It was at this moment that Andrée, returning from the Opéra-Comique, looked at Gigi's dishevelled head rolling against Lachaille's sleeve and saw the tears of excited laughter in her lovely slate-blue eyes. She said nothing, and accepted a glass of champagne, then another, and yet another. After her third glass, Gaston Lachaille was threatened with the Bell Song from *Lakmé*, at which point her mother led her away to bed.

The following day, no one spoke of this family party except Gilberte, who exclaimed, 'Never, never in all my life, have I laughed so much! And the pencil-case is real gold!' Her unre-served chatter met with a strange silence, or rather with 'Now then, Gigi, try to be a little more serious!' thrown out almost absent-mindedly.

After that, Gaston Lachaille let a fortnight go by without giv- 25 ing any sign of life, and the Alvarez family gathered its information from the papers only.

'Did you see, Andrée? In the Gossip Column it says that Monsieur Gaston Lachaille has left for Monte Carlo. *The reason for this seems to be of a sentimental nature—a secret that we respect.* What next!'

'Would you believe it, Grandmamma. Lydia Poret was saying at the dancing class that Liane travelled on the same train as Tonton, but in another compartment! Grandmamma, do you think it can be true?'

Madame Alvarez shrugged her shoulders.

'If it was true, how on earth would those Porets know? Have they become friends with Monsieur Lachaille all of a sudden?'

'No, but Lydia Poret heard the story in her aunt's dressing-room at the Comédie Française.'

Madame Alvarez exchanged looks with her daughter.

'In her dressing-room! That explains everything!' she exclaimed, for she held the theatrical profession in contempt, although Andrée worked so hard. When Madame Émilienne d'Alençon had decided to present performing rabbits, and Madame de Pougy—shyer on the stage than any young girl—had amused herself by miming the part of Columbine in spangled black tulle, Madame Alvarez had stigmatized them both in a single phrase. 'What! have they sunk to that?'

'Grandmamma, tell me, Grandmamma, do you know him, this Prince Radziwill?' Gilberte went on again.

'What's come over the child today? Has she been bitten by a flea? Which Prince Radziwill, to begin with? There's more than one.'

'I don't know,' said Gigi. 'The one who's getting married.

Among the list of presents, it says here, *"are three writing-sets in malachite"*. What is malachite?'

'Oh, you're being tiresome, child. If he's getting married, he's no longer interesting.'

'But if Tonton got married, wouldn't he be interesting either?'

'It all depends. It would be interesting if he were to marry his mistress. When Prince Cheniaguine married Valérie d'Aigreville, it was obvious that the life she had led for him for the past fifteen years was all he wanted; scenes, plates flung across the room, and reconciliations in the middle of the Restaurant Durand, Place de la Madeleine. Clearly, she was a woman who knew how to make herself valued. But all that is too complicated for you, my poor Gigi.'

'And do you think it's to marry Liane that they've gone away together?'

Madame Alvarez pressed her forehead against the window-pane, and seemed to be consulting the spring sunshine, which bestowed upon the street a bright side and a shady one.

'No,' she said, 'not if I know anything about anything. I must have a word with Alicia. Gigi, come with me as far as her house; you can leave me there and find your way back along the quais. It will give you some fresh air, since, it would seem, one must have fresh air nowadays I have never been in the habit of taking the air more than twice a year, myself, at Cabourg and at Monte Carlo. And I am none the worse for that.'

That evening Madame Alvarez came in so late that the family dined off tepid soup, cold meat, and some cakes sent round by Aunt Alicia. To Gilberte's 'Well, what did she have to say?' she presented an icy front, and replied in clarion tones:

'She says she is going to teach you how to eat ortolans.' 27

'Scrumptious!' cried Gilberte. 'And what did she say about the summer frock she promised me?'

'She said she would see. And that's no reason why you should be displeased with the result.'

'Oh!' said Gilberte gloomily.

'She also wants you to go to luncheon with her on Thursday, sharp at twelve.'

'With you, too, Grandmamma?'

Madame Alvarez looked at the willowy slip of a girl facing her across the table, at her high, rosy cheekbones beneath eyes as blue as an evening sky, at her strong even teeth biting a fresh-coloured but slightly chapped lip, and at the primitive splendour of her ash-gold hair.

'No,' she said at last. 'Without me.'

Gilberte got up and wound an arm about her grandmother's neck.

'The way you said that, Grandmamma, surely doesn't mean that you're going to send me live with Aunt Alicia? I don't want to leave here, Grandmamma!'

Madame Alvarez cleared her throat, gave a little cough and smiled.

"Goodness gracious, what a foolish creature you are! Leave here! Why, my poor Gigi, I'm not scolding you, but you've not reached the first stage towards leaving.'

For a bell-pull, Aunt Alicia had hung from her front door a length of bead-embroidered braid on the background of twining green vine-leaves and purple grapes. The door itself, varnished and revarnished till it glistened, shone with the glow of a dark-brown caramel. From the very threshold, where she was admitted by a 'man-servant', Gilberte enjoyed in her undiscriminating

way an atmosphere of discreet luxury. The carpet, spread with Persian rugs, seemed to lend her wings. After hearing Madame Alvarez pronounce her sister's Louis XV little drawing-room to be 'boredom itself', Gilberte echoed her words by saying: 'Aunt Alicia's drawing-room is very pretty, but it's boredom itself!' reserving her admiration for the dining room, furnished in pale almost golden lemon wood dating from the Directoire, quite plain but for the grain of a wood as transparent as wax. 'I shall buy myself a set like that one day,' Gigi had once said in all innocence.

'In the Faubourg Antoine, I dare say,' Aunt Alicia had answered teasingly, with a smile of her cupid's bow mouth and a flash of small teeth.

She was seventy years old. Her fastidious taste was everywhere apparent; in her silver-grey bedroom with its red Chinese vases, in her narrow white bathroom as warm as a hot-house, and in her robust health, concealed by a pretence of delicacy. The men of her generation, when trying to describe Alicia de Saint-Efflam, fumbled for words and could only exclaim, 'Oh, my dear fellow!' or 'Nothing could give you the faintest ideah!' Those who had known her intimately produced photographs which younger men found ordinary enough. 'Was she really so lovely? You wouldn't think so from her photographs!' Looking at portraits of her, old admirers would pause for an instant, recollecting the turn of a wrist like a swan's neck, the tiny ear, the profile revealing a delicious kinship between the heart-shaped mouth and the wide-cut eyelids with their long lashes.

Gilberte kissed the pretty old lady, who was wearing a peak of black Chantilly lace on her white hair, and, on her slightly dumpy figure, a tea-gown of shot taffeta.

'You have one of your headaches, Aunt Alicia?'

'I'm not sure yet,' replied Aunt Alicia; 'it depends on the luncheon. Come quickly; the eggs are ready! Take off your coat! What on earth is that dress?'

'One of Mamma's, altered to fit me. Are they difficult eggs today?'

'Not at all. *Œufs brouillés aux croutons*. The ortolans are not difficult, either. And you shall have chocolate cream. So shall I.'

With her young voice, a touch of pink on her amiable wrinkles, and lace on her white hair, Aunt Alicia was the perfect stage marquise. Gilberte had the greatest reverence for her aunt. In sitting down to table in her presence, she would pull her skirt up behind, join her knees, hold her elbows close to her sides, straighten her shoulder-blades, and to all appearances become the perfect young lady. She would remember what she had been taught, break her bread quietly, eat with her mouth shut, and take care, when cutting her meat, not to let her forefinger reach the blade of her knife.

Today her hair, severely tied back in a heavy knot at the nape of her neck, disclosed the fresh line of her forehead and ears, and a very powerful throat, rising from the rather ill-cut opening of her altered dress. This was a dingy blue, the bodice pleated about a let-in piece and, to cheer up this patchwork, three rows of mohair braid had been sewn round the hem of the skirt, and three times three rows of mohair braid round the sleeves, between the wrist and elbow.

Aunt Alicia, sitting opposite her niece and examining her through fine dark eyes, could find no fault.

'How old are you?' she asked suddenly.

'The same as I was the other day, Aunt. Fifteen and a half. Aunt, what do you really think of this business of Tonton
Gaston?'

'Why? Does it interest you?'

'Of course, Aunt. It worries me. If Tonton takes up with another lady, he won't come and play piquet with us any more or drink camomile tea—at least not for some time. That would be a shame.'

'That's one way of looking at it, certainly.'

Aunt Alicia examined her niece critically, through narrowed eyelids.

'Do you work hard, in class? Who are your friends? Ortolans should be cut in two, with one quick stroke of the knife, and no grating of the blade on the plate. Bite up each half. The bones don't matter. Go on eating while you answer my question, but don't talk with your mouth full. You must manage it. If I can, you can. What friends have you made?'

'None, Aunt. Grandmamma won't even let me have tea with the families of my school friends.'

'She is quite right. Apart from that, there is no one who follows you, no little clerk hanging round your skirts? No schoolboy? No older man? I warn you, I shall know at once if you lie to me.'

Gilberte gazed at the bright face of the imperious old lady who was questioning her so sharply.

'Why, no, Aunt, no one. Has somebody been telling you tales about me? I am always on my own. And why does Grandmamma stop me from accepting invitations?'

'She is right, for once. You would only be invited by ordinary people—that is to say, useless people.'

'And what about us? Aren't we ordinary people ourselves?'

'No.'

'What makes these ordinary people inferior to us?'

'They have weak heads and dissolute bodies. Besides, they are married. But I don't think you understand.'

'Yes. Aunt, I understand that we don't marry.'

'Marriage is not forbidden to us. Instead of marrying "at once", it sometimes happens that we marry "at last".'

'But does that prevent me from seeing girls of my own age?'

'Yes. Are you bored at home? Well, be a little bored. It's not a bad thing. Boredom helps one to make decisions. What is the matter? Tears? The tears of a silly child who is backward for her age. Have another ortolan.'

Aunt Alicia, with three glittering fingers, grasped the stem of her glass and raised it in a toast.

"To you and me, Gigi! You shall have an Egyptian cigarette with your coffee. On condition that you do not make the end of it wet, and that you don't spit out specks of tobacco—going *ptu*, *ptu*. I shall also give you a note to the *première vendeuse* at Béchoff-David, an old friend of mine who was not a success. Your wardrobe is going to be changed. Nothing venture, nothing have.'

The dark-blue eyes gleamed. Gilberte stammered with joy.

'Aunt! Aunt! I'm going to . . . to Bé—'

'—choff-David. But I thought you weren't interested in clothes?'

Gilberte blushed.

'Aunt, I'm not interested in home-made clothes.'

'I sympathize with you. Can it be that you have taste? When you think of looking your best, how do you see yourself dressed?'

'Oh, but I know just what would suit me, Aunt! I've seen—'

'Explain yourself without gestures. The moment you gesticu-
late you look common.'

'I've seen a dress . . . oh, a dress created for Madame Lucy Gérard! Myriads of tiny ruffles of pearl-grey silk muslin from top to bottom. And then a dress of lavender-blue cloth cut out on a black velvet foundation, the cut-out design making a sort of peacock's tail on the train.'

The small hand with its precious stones flashed through the air.

'Enough! Enough! I see your fancy is to be dressed like a leading *comédienne* at the Théâtre Français—and don't take that as a compliment! Come and pour out the coffee. And without jerking up the lip of the coffee-pot to prevent the drop from falling. I'd rather have a foot-bath in my saucer than see you juggling like a waiter in a café.'

The next hour passed very quickly for Gilberte: Aunt Alicia had unlocked her casket of jewels to use for a lesson that dazzled her.

'What is that, Gigi?'

'A marquise diamond.'

'We say, a marquise-shaped brilliant. And that?'

'A topaz.'

Aunt Alicia threw up her hands and the sunlight, glancing off her rings, set off a myriad scintillations.

'A topaz! I have suffered many humiliations, but this surpasses them all. A topaz among my jewels! Why not an aquamarine or a chrysolite? It's a jonquil diamond, little goose, and you won't often see its like. And this?'

Gilberte half-opened her mouth, as though in a dream.

'Oh! That's an emerald. Oh, how beautiful it is!'

Aunt Alicia slipped the large square-cut emerald on one of her thin fingers and was lost in silence.

'Do you see,' she said in a hushed voice, 'that almost blue

flame darting about in the depths of the green light? Only the most beautiful emeralds contain that miracle of elusive blue.'

'Who gave it to you, Aunt?' Gilberte dared to ask.

'A king,' said Aunt Alicia simply.

'A great king?'

'No. A little one. Great kings do not give very fine stones.'

'Why not?'

For a fleeting moment, Aunt Alicia proferred a glimpse of her tiny white teeth.

'If you want my opinion, it's because they don't want to. Between ourselves, the little ones don't either.'

'Then who does give great big stones?'

'Who? The shy. The proud, too. And the bounders, because they think that to give a monster jewel is a sign of good breeding. Sometimes a woman does, to humiliate a man. Never wear second-rate jewels; wait till the really good ones come to you.'

'And if they don't?'

'Well, then it can't be helped. Rather than a wretched hundred-guinea diamond, wear a half-crown ring. In that case you can say, "It's a memento. I never part with it, day or night." Don't ever wear artistic jewellery; it wrecks a woman's reputation."

'What is an artistic jewel?'

'It all depends. A mermaid in gold, with eyes of chrysoprase. An Egyptian scarab. A large engraved amethyst. A not very heavy bracelet said to have been chased by a master-hand. A lyre or star, mounted as a brooch. A studded tortoise. In a word, all of them frightful. Never wear baroque pearls, not even as hat-pins. Beware above all things, of family jewels!'

'But Grandmamma has a beautiful cameo, set as a medallion.'

'There are no beautiful cameos,' said Aunt Alicia with a toss of the head. 'There are precious stones and pearls. There are white, yellow, blue, blue-white, or pink diamonds. We won't speak of black diamonds, they're not worth mentioning. Then there are rubies—when you can be sure of them; sapphires, when they come from Kashmir; emeralds, provided they have no fatal flaw, or are not too light in colour, or have a yellowish tint.'

'Aunt, I am very fond of opals, too.'

'I am very sorry, but you are not to wear them. I won't allow it.'

Dumbfounded, Gilberte remained for a moment open-mouthed.

'Oh! Do you too, Aunt, really believe that they bring bad luck?'

'Why in the world not? You silly little creature,' Alicia went bubbling on, 'you must pretend to believe in such things. Believe in opals, believe—let's see, what can I suggest—in turquoises that die, in the evil eye . . .'

'But,' said Gigi, haltingly, 'those are . . . are superstitions!'

'Of course they are, child. They also go by the name of weaknesses. A pretty little collection of weaknesses and a terror of spiders are our indispensable stock-in-trade with the men.'

'Why, Aunt?'

The old lady closed the casket, and kept Gilberte kneeling before her.

'Because nine men out of ten are superstitious, nineteen out of twenty believe in the evil eye, and ninety eight out of a hundred are afraid of spiders. They forgive us—oh! for many things, but not for the absence in us of their own feelings. What makes you sigh?'

'I shall never remember all that!'

'The important thing is not for you to remember, but for me to know it.'

'Aunt, what is a writing-set in . . . in malachite?'

'Always a calamity. But where on earth did you pick up such terms?'

'From the list of presents at grand weddings, Aunt, printed in the papers.'

'Nice reading! But, at least you can gather from it what kind of presents you should never give or accept.'

While speaking, she began to touch here and there the young face on a level with her own, with the sharp pointed nail of her index finger. She lifted one slightly chapped lip, inspected the spotless enamel of the teeth.

'A fine jaw, my girl! With such teeth, I should have gobbled up Paris, and the rest of the world into the bargain. As it was, I had a good bite out of it. What's this you've got here? A small pimple? You shouldn't have a small pimple near your nose. And this? You've squeezed a blackhead. You've no business to have such things, or to squeeze them. I'll give you some of my astringent lotion. You mustn't eat anything from the pork-butcher's except cooked ham. You don't put on powder?'

'Grandmamma won't let me.'

'I should hope not. . . . Let me smell your breath. Not that it means anything at his hour, you've just had luncheon.'

She laid her hands on Gigi's shoulders.

'Pay attention to what I'm going to say. You have it in your power to please. You have an impossible little nose, a nondescript mouth, cheeks rather like the wife of a *moujik*—'

'Oh, Aunt!' sighed Gilberte.

'But, with your eyes and eyelashes, your teeth, and your hair, you can get away with it, if you're not a perfect fool. As for the

rest—'

She cupped her hands like conch-shells over Gigi's bosom and smiled.

'A promise, but a pretty promise, neatly moulded. Don't eat too many almonds; they add weight to the breasts. Ah! remind me to teach you how to choose cigars.'

Gilberte opened her eyes so wide that the tips of her lashes touched her eyebrows.

'Why?'

She received a little tap on the cheek.

'Because—because I do nothing without good reason. If I take you in hand at all, I must do it thoroughly. Once a woman understands the tastes of a man, cigars included, and once a man knows what pleases a woman, they may be said to be well matched.'

'And then they fight,' concluded Gigi with a knowing air.

'What do you mean, they fight?'

The old lady looked at Gigi in consternation.

'Ah!' she added, 'you certainly never invented the triple mirror! Come, you little psychologist! Let me give you a note for Madame Henriette at Béchoff.'

While her aunt was writing at a miniature rose-pink escritoire, Gilberte breathed in the scent of the fastidiously furnished room. Without wanting them for herself, she examined the objects she knew so well but hardly appreciated: Cupid, the Archer, pointing to the hours on the mantelpiece; two rather daring pictures; a bed like the basin of a fountain and its chinchilla coverlet; a rosary of small seed pearls and the New Testament on the bedside table; two red Chinese vases fitted as lamps—a happy note against the grey of the walls.

'Run along, my little one. I shall send for you again quite soon. Don't forget to ask Victor for the cake you're to take 37 home. Gently, don't disarrange my hair! And remember, I shall have my eye on you as you leave the house. Woe betide you if you march like a guardsman, or drag your feet behind you!'

The month of May fetched Gaston Lachaille back to Paris, and brought to Gilberte two well-cut dresses and a light-weight coat—'a sack-coat like Cléo de Mérode's' she called it—as well as hats and boots and shoes. To these she added, on her own account, a few curls over the forehead, which cheapened her appearance. She paraded in front of Gaston in a blue-and-white dress reaching almost to the ground. 'A full seven and a half yards round, Tonton, my skirt measures!' She was more than proud of her slender waist, held in by a grosgrain sash with a silver buckle; but she tried every dodge to free her lovely strong neck from its whale-bone collar of 'imitation Venetian point' which matched the tucks of her bodice. The full sleeves and wide-flounced skirt of blue-and-white striped silk rustled deliciously, and Gilberte delighted in pecking at her sleeves, to puff them out just below the shoulder.

'You remind me of a performing monkey,' Lachaille said to her. 'I liked you much better in your old tartan dress. In that uncomfortable collar you look just like a hen with a full crop. Take a peep at yourself!'

Feeling a little ruffled, Gilberte turned round to face the looking-glass. She had a lump in one of her cheeks caused by a large caramel, out of a box sent all the way from Nice at Gaston's order.

'I've heard a good deal about you, Tonton,' she retorted, 'but I've never heard it said that you had any taste in clothes.'

He started, almost choking, at this newly-fledged young
woman, then turned to Madame Alvarez.

'Charming manners you've taught her! I congratulate you!'

Whereupon he left the house without drinking his camomile tea, and Madame Alvarez wrung her hands.

'Look what you've done for us now, my poor Gigi!'

'I know,' said Gigi, 'but then why does he go for me? He must know by now, I should think, that I can give as good as I get!'

Her grandmother shook her by the arm.

'But think what you've done, you wretched child! Good heavens! when will you learn to think? You've mortally offended the man, as likely as not. Just when we are doing our utmost to—'

'To do what, Grandmamma?'

'Why! to do everything to make an elegant young lady of you, to show you off to advantage.'

'For whose benefit, Grandmamma? You must admit that one doesn't have to turn oneself inside out for an old friend like Tonton!'

But Madame Alvarez admitted nothing: not even to her astonishment, when, the following day, Gaston Lachaille arrived in the best of spirits, wearing a light-coloured suit.

'Put on your hat, Gigi! I'm taking you out to tea.'

'Where?' cried Gigi.

'To the *Réservoirs*, at Versailles!'

'Hurrah!! Hurrah! Hurrah!' chanted Gilberte.

She turned towards the kitchen.

'Grandmamma, I'm having tea at the *Réservoirs*, with Tonton!'

Madame Alvarez appeared, and without stopping to untie the flowered satinette apron across her stomach, interposed her soft hand between Gilberte's arm and that of Gaston Lachaille.

'No, Gaston,' she said simply.

'What do you mean, No?'

'Oh, Grandmamma!' wailed Gigi.

39

Madame Alvarez seemed not to hear her.

'Go to your room a minute, Gigi! I should like to talk to Monsieur Lachaille in private.'

She watched Gilberte leave the room and close the door behind her; then, returning to Gaston, she met his dark rather brutal stare without flinching.

'What is the meaning of all this, Mamita? Ever since yesterday, I find quite a change here. What's going on?'

'I shall be glad if you will sit down, Gaston. I'm tired,' said Madame Alvarez. 'Oh, my poor legs!'

She sighed, waited for a response that did not come, and then untied her apron, under which she was wearing a black dress with a large cameo pinned upon it. She motioned her guest to a high-backed chair, keeping the armchair for herself. Then she sat down heavily, smoothed her greying black coils, and folded her hands on her lap. The unhurried movement of her large, dark, lambent eyes, and the ease with which she remained motionless, were sure signs of her self-control.

'Gaston, you cannot doubt my friendship for you.' Lachaille emitted a short, businesslike laugh, and tugged at his moustache. 'My friendship and my gratitude. Nevertheless, I must never forget that I have a soul entrusted to my care. Andrée, as you know, has neither the time nor the inclination to look after the girl. Our Gilberte has not got the gumption to make her own way in the world, like so many. She is just a child.'

'Of sixteen,' said Lachaille.

'Of nearly sixteen,' consented Madame Alvarez. 'For years you have been giving her sweets and playthings. She swears by Tonton, and by him alone. And now you want to take her out to tea, in your automobile, to the *Réservoirs!*'

40   Madame Alvarez placed a hand on her heart.

'Upon my soul and conscience, Gaston, if there were only you and me, I should say to you, "Take Gilberte anywhere you like, I entrust her to you blindly." But there are always the others. The eyes of the world are on you. To be seen *tête-à-tête* with you, is, for a woman—'

Gaston Lachaille lost patience.

'All right, all right. I understand. You want me to believe that once she is seen having tea with me, Gilberte is compromised! A slip of a girl, a flapper, a chit whom no one notices!'

'Let us say rather,' interrupted Madame Alvarez gently, 'that she will be labelled. No matter where you put in an appearance, Gaston, your presence is remarked upon. A young girl who goes out alone with you is no longer an ordinary girl, or even—to put it bluntly—a respectable girl. Now our little Gilberte must not, above all things, cease to be an ordinary young girl, at least not by that method. So far as it concerns you, it will simply end in one more story to be added to the long list already in existence, but personally, when I read of it in *Gil Blas*, I shall not be amused.'

Gaston Lachaille rose, paced from the table to the door, then from the door to the window, before replying.

'Very good, Mamita, I have no wish to vex you. I shan't argue,' he said coldly. 'Keep your precious child.'

He turned round again to face Madame Alvarez, his chin held high.

'I can't help wondering, as a matter of interest, whom you are keeping her for! A clerk earning a hundred a year, who'll marry her and give her four children in three years?'

'I know the duty of a mother better than that,' said Madame Alvarez composedly. 'I shall do my best to entrust Gigi only to the care of a man capable of saying, "I take charge of her and 41 answer for her future." May I have the pleasure of brewing you some camomile tea, Gaston?'

'No, thank you, I'm late already.'

'Would you like Gigi to come and say goodbye?'

'Don't bother. I'll see her another time. I can't say when, I'm sure. I'm very much taken up these days.'

'Never mind, Gaston; don't worry about her. Have a good time, Gaston.'

Once alone, Madame Alvarez mopped her forehead and went to open the door of Gilberte's room.

'You were listening at the door, Gigi!'

'No, Grandmamma.'

'Yes, you had your ear to the key-hole. You must never listen at key-holes. You don't hear properly and so you get things all wrong. Monsieur Lachaille has gone.'

'So I can see,' said Gilberte.

'Now you must rub the new potatoes in a cloth; I'll sauté them when I come in.'

'Are you going out, Grandmamma?'

'I'm going round to see Alicia.'

'Again?'

'Is it your place to object?' said Madame Alvarez severely. 'You had better bathe your eyes in cold water, since you have been silly enough to cry.'

'Grandmamma!'

'What?'

'What difference could it make to you, if you'd let me go out with Tonton Gaston in my new dress?'

'Silence! If you can't understand anything about anything, at
least let those who are capable of using their reason do so for

you. And put on my rubber gloves before you touch the potatoes!'

Throughout the whole of the following week, silence reigned over the Alvarez household, except for a surprise visit, one day, from Aunt Alicia. She arrived in a hired brougham, all black lace and dull silk with a rose at her shoulder, and carried on an anxious conversation, strictly between themselves, with her younger sister. As she was leaving, she bestowed only a moment's attention on Gilberte, pecked at her cheek with a fleeting kiss, and was gone.

'What did she want?' Gilberte asked Madame Alvarez.

'Oh, nothing ... the address of the heart specialist who treated Madame Buffetery.'

Gilberte reflected for a moment.

'It was a lengthy one,' she said.

'What was lengthy?'

'The address of the heart specialist. Grandmamma, I should like a *cachet*. I have a headache.'

'But you had one yesterday. A headache doesn't last forty-eight hours!'

'Presumably my headaches are different from other people's,' said Gilberte, offended.

She was losing some of her sweetness, and, on her return from school, would make some such remark as 'My teacher has got his knife into me!' or complain of not being able to sleep. She was gradually slipping into a state of idleness, which her grandmother noticed, but did nothing to overcome.

One day Gigi was busy applying liquid chalk to her white canvas button boots, when Gaston Lachaille put in an appearance without ringing the bell. His hair was too long, his com- 43 plexion sun-tanned, and he was wearing a broad check summer suit. He stopped short in front of Gilberte, who was perched high on a kitchen stool, her left hand shod with a boot.

'Oh! Grandmamma left the key in the door. That's just like her!'

As Gaston Lachaille looked at her without saying a word, she began to blush, put down the boot on the table and pulled her skirt down over her knees.

'So, Tonton, you slip in like a burglar! I belive you're thinner. Aren't you fed properly by that famous chef of yours who used to be with the Prince of Wales? Being thinner makes your eyes look larger, and at the same time makes your nose longer, and—'

'I have something to say to your grandmother,' interrupted Gaston Lachaille, 'Run into you room, Gigi!'

For a moment she remained open-mouthed; then she jumped off her stool. The strong column of her neck, like an archangel's, swelled with anger as she advanced upon Lachaille.

'Run into your room! Run into your room! And suppose I said the same to you? Who do you think you are here, ordering me to run into my room? All right, I'm going to my room! And I can tell you one thing; so long as you're in the house, I shan't come out of it!'

She slammed the door behind her, and there was a dramatic click of the bolt.

'Gaston,' breathed Madame Alvarez. 'I shall insist on the child apologizing. Yes, I shall insist. If necessary, I'll . . .'

Gaston was not listening to her, and stood staring at the closed door.

'Now, Mamita,' said he, 'let us talk briefly and to the point.'

44   * * *

'Let us go over it all once again,' said Aunt Alicia. 'To begin with, you are quite sure he said, "She shall be spoiled, more than—" '

'Than any woman before her!'

'Yes, but that's the sort of vague phrase that every man comes out with. I like things cut and dried.'

'Just what they were, Alicia, for he said the he would guarantee Gigi against every imaginable mishap, even against himself, by an insurance policy; and that he regarded himself more or less as her godfather.'

'Yes, yes. Not bad, not bad. But vague, vague as ever.'

She was still in her bed, her white hair arranged in curls against the pink pillow. She was absent-mindedly tying and untying the ribbon of her nightdress. Madame Alvarez, pale, and as wan under her mourning hat as the moon behind the passing clouds, was leaning cross-armed against the bedside.

'And he added, "I don't wish to rush anything. Above all, I am Gigi's best pal. I shall give her all the time she wants to get used to me." There were tears in his eyes. And he also said, "After all, she won't have to deal with a savage." A gentleman, in fact. A perfect gentleman.'

'Yes, yes. Rather a vague gentleman. And the child, have you spoken frankly to her?'

'As was my duty, Alicia. This is no time for us to be treating her like a child from whom the cakes have to be hidden. Yes, I spoke to her frankly. I referred to Gaston as a miracle, as a god, as—'

'Tut, tut, tut,' criticized Alicia. 'I should have stressed the difficulties rather: the cards to be played, the fury of all those ladies, the conquest represented by so conspicuous a man.'

Madame Alvarez wrung her hands.

'The difficulties! The cards to be played! Do you imagine she's like you? Don't you know her at all? She's very far from calculating; she's—'

'Thank you.'

'I mean she has no ambition. I was even struck by the fact that she did not react either one way or the other. No cries of joy, no tears of emotion! All I got from her was. "Oh, yes! Oh, it's very considerate of him." Then, only at the very end, did she lay down as her conditions—'

'Conditions, indeed!' murmured Alicia.

'—that she would answer Monsieur Lachaille's proposals herself, and discuss the matter alone with him. In other words, it was her business, and hers only.'

'Let us be prepared for the worst! You've brought a half-wit into the world. She will ask for the moon and, if I know him, she won't get it. He is coming at four o'clock?'

'Yes.'

'Hasn't he sent anything? No flowers? No little present?'

'Nothing. Do you think that's a bad sign?'

'No. It's what one would expect. See that the child is nicely dressed. How is she looking?'

'Not too well today. Poor little lamb—'

'Come, come!' said Alicia heartlessly. 'You'll have time for tears another day—when she's succeeded in wrecking the whole affair.'

'You've eaten scarcely anything, Gigi.'

'I wasn't too hungry, Grandmamma. May I have a little more coffee?'

'Of course.'

'And a drop of Combier?'

'Why, yes. There's nothing in the world better than Combier for settling the stomach.'

Through the open window rose the noise and heat from the street below. Gigi let the tip of her tongue lick round the bottom of her liqueur glass.

'If Aunt Alicia could see you, Gigi!' said Madame Alvarez lightheartedly.

Gigi's only reply was a disillusioned little smile. Her old plaid dress was too tight across the breast, and under the table she stretched out her long legs well beyond the limits of her skirt.

"What can Mamma be rehearsing today that's kept her from coming back to eat with us, Grandmamma? Do you think there really is a rehearsal going on at her Opéra-Comique?'

'She said so, didn't she?'

'Personally, I don't think she wanted to eat here.'

'What makes you think that?'

Without taking her eyes off the sunny window, Gigi simply shrugged her shoulders.

'Oh, nothing, Grandmamma.'

When she had drained the last drop of her Combier, she rose and began to clear the table.

'Leave all that, Gigi. I'll do it.'

'Why, Grandmamma? I do it as a rule.'

She looked Madame Alvarez straight in the face, with an expression the old lady could not meet.

'We began our meal late, it's almost three o'clock and you're not dressed yet. Do pull yourself together, Gigi.'

'It's never before taken me a whole hour to change my clothes.'

'Won't you need my help? Are you satisfied your hair's all right?'

'It will do, Grandmamma. When the door-bell rings, don't bother, I'll go and open it.'

On the stroke of four, Gaston Lachaille rang three times. A childish, wistful face looked out from the bed-room door, listening. After three more impatient rings, Gilberte advanced as far as the middle of the hall. She still had on her old plaid dress and cotton stockings. She rubbed her cheeks with both fists, then ran to open the door.

'Good afternoon, Uncle Gaston.'

'Didn't you want to let me in, you bad girl?'

They bumped shoulders in passing through the door, said, 'Oh, sorry!' a little too self-consciously, then laughed awkwardly.

'Please sit down, Tonton. D'you know, I didn't have time to change. Not like you! That navy blue serge couldn't look better!'

'You don't know what your talking about! It's tweed.'

'Of course. How silly of me!'

She sat down facing him, pulled her skirt over her knees, and they stared at each other. Gilberte's tomboy assurance deserted her; a strange woebegone look made her blue eyes seem twice their natural size.

'What's the matter with you, Gigi?' asked Lachaille softly. 'Tell me something! Do you know why I'm here?'

She assented with an exaggerated nod.

'Do you want to, or don't you?' he asked, lowering his voice.

She pushed a curl behind her ear, and swallowed bravely.

'I don't want to.'

Lachaille twirled the tips of his moustache between two fingers, and for a moment looked away from a pair of darkened blue eyes, a pink cheek with a single freckle, curved lashes, a mouth unaware of its power, a heavy mass of ash-gold hair, and a neck as straight as a column, strong, hardly feminine, all of a piece, innocent of jewellery.

'I don't want what you want,' Gilberte began again. 'You said to Grandmamma . . .'

He put out his hand to stop her. His mouth slightly twisted to one side, as if he had the toothache.

'I know what I said to your grandmother. It's not worth repeating. Just tell me what it is you don't want. You can then tell me what you do want. I shall give it to you.'

'You mean that?' cried Gilberte.

He nodded, letting his shoulders droop, as if tired out. She watched with surprise, these signs of exhaustion and torment.

'Tonton, you told Grandmamma you wanted to make me my fortune.'

'A very fine one,' said Lachaille firmly.

'It will be fine if I like it,' said Gilberte, no less firmly. 'They've drummed it into my ears that I am backward for my age, but all the same I know the meaning of words. "Make me my fortune": that means I should go away from here with you, and that I should sleep in your bed.'

'Gigi, I beg of you!'

She stopped because of the strong note of appeal in his voice.

'But, Tonton, why should I mind speaking of it to you? You didn't mind speaking of it to Grandmamma. Neither did Grandmamma mind speaking of it to me. Grandmamma wanted me to see nothing but the bright side. But I know more than she told me. I know very well that if you make me my fortune, then I must have my photograph in the papers, go to the Battle of Flowers and to the races at Deauville. When we quarrel, *Gil Blas* and *Paris en amour* will tell the whole story. When you 49 throw me over once and for all, as you did Gentiane des Cevennes when you'd had enough of her—'

'What! You've heard about that? They've bothered your head with all those old stories?'

She gave a solemn little nod.

'Grandmamma and Aunt Alicia. They've taught me that you're world-famous. I know too that Maryse Chuquet stole your letters, and you brought an action against her. I know that Countess Pariewsky was angry with you because you didn't want to marry a *divorcée*, and she tried to shoot you. I know what all the world knows.'

Lachaille put his hand on Gilberte's knee.

'Those are not things we have to talk about together, Gigi. All that's in the past. All that's over and done with.'

'Of course, Tonton, until it begins again. It's not your fault if you're world-famous. But I haven't got a world-famous sort of nature. So it won't do for me.'

In pulling at the hem of her skirt, she caused Lachaille's hand to slip off her knee.

'Aunt Alicia and Grandmamma are on your side. But as it concerns me a little, after all, I think you must allow me to say a word on the subject. And my word is, that it won't do for me.'

She got up and walked about the room. Gaston Lachailles' silence seemed to embarrass her. She punctuated her wanderings with 'After all, it's true, I suppose! No, it really won't do!'

'I should like to know,' said Gaston at last, 'whether you're not just trying to hide from me the fact that you dislike me. If you dislike me, you had better say so at once.'

'Oh no, Tonton, I don't dislike you at all! I'm always delighted to see you! I'll prove it by making a suggestion in my turn. You could go on coming here as usual, even more often.

No one would see any harm in it, since you're a friend of the family. You could go on bringing me liquorice, champagne on my birthdays, and on Sunday we should have an extra special game of piquet. Wouldn't that be a pleasant little life? A life without all this business of sleeping in your bed and everybody knowing about it, losing strings of pearls, being photographed all the time and having to be so careful.'

She was absent-mindedly twisting a strand of her hair round her nose, and pulled it so tight that she snuffled and the tip of her nose turned purple.

'A very pretty little life, as you say,' interrupted Gaston Lachaille. 'You're forgetting one thing only, Gigi, and that is, I'm in love with you.'

'Oh!' she cried. 'You never told me that.'

'Well,' he answered uneasily. 'I'm telling you now.'

She remained standing before him, silent and breathing fast. There was no concealing her embarrassment; the rise and fall of her bosom under the tight bodice, the high colour on her cheeks, and the quivering of her close-pressed lips—albeit ready to open again and taste of life.

'That's quite another thing!' she cried at last. 'But then you are a terrible man! You're in love with me, and you want to drag me into a life where I'll have nothing but worries, where everyone gossips about everyone else, where the papers print nasty stories. You're in love with me, and you don't care a fig if you let me fall in for all sorts of horrible adventures, ending in separations, quarrels, Sandomirs, revolvers, and lau . . . and laudanum.'

She burst into violent sobs, which made as much noise as a fit of coughing. Gaston put his arms round her to bend her towards him like a branch, but she escaped and took refuge between the wall and the piano.

'But listen, Gigi! Listen to me!'

'Never! I never want to see you again! I should never have believed it of you. You're not in love with me, you're a wicked man! Go away from here!'

She shut him out from sight by rubbing her eyes with closed fists. Gaston had moved over to her and was trying to discover some place on her well-guarded face where he could kiss her. But his lips found only the point of a small chin wet with tears. At the sound of sobbing, Madame Alvarez had hurried in. Pale and circumspect, she had stopped in hesitation at the door to the kitchen.

'Good gracious, Gaston!' she said. 'What on earth's the matter with her?'

'The matter!' said Lachaille. 'The matter is that she doesn't want to.'

She doesn't want to!' repeated Madame Alvarez. 'What do you mean, she doesn't want to?'

'No, she doesn't want to. I speak plainly enough, don't I?'

'No. I don't want to,' whimpered Gigi.

Madame Alvarez looked at her granddaughter in a sort of terror.

'Gigi! It's enough to drive one raving mad! But I told you, Gigi. Gaston, as God is my witness, I told her—'

'You have told her too much!' cried Lachaille.

He turned his face towards the child, looking just a poor, sad, lovesick creature, but all he saw of her was a slim back shaken by sobs and a dishevelled head of hair.

'Oh!' he exclaimed hoarsely. 'I've had enough of this!' And he 52 went out, banging the door.

The next day, at three o'clock, Aunt Alicia, summoned by *pneumatique*, stepped out from her hired brougham. She climbed the stairs up to the Alvarez' floor—pretending to the shortness of breath proper to someone with a weak heart—and noiselessly pushed open the door, which her sister had left on the latch.

'Where's the child?'

'In her room. Do you want to see her?'

'There's plenty of time. How is she?'

'Very calm.'

Alicia shook two angry little fists.

'Very calm! She has pulled the roof down about our heads, and she is very calm! These young people of today!'

Once again she raised her spotted veil and withered her sister with a single glance.

'And you, standing there, what do you propose doing?'

With a face like a crumpled rose, she sternly confronted the large pallid face of her sister, whose retort was mild in the extreme.

'What do I propose doing? How do you mean? I can't after all, tie the child up!' Her burdened shoulders rose on a long sigh. 'I surely have not deserved such children as these!'

'While you stand there wringing your hands, Lachaille has rushed away from here and in such a state that he may do something idiotic!'

'And even without his straw hat,' said Madame Alvarez. 'He got into his motor bare-headed! The whole street might have seen him!'

'If I were to be told that by this time he's already become engaged, or is busy making it up with Liane, it would not surprise me in the least!'

'It is a moment fraught with destiny,' said Madame Alvarez lugubriously.

'And afterwards, how did you speak to that little chit?'

Madame Alvarez pursed her lips.

'Gigi may be a bit scatter-brained in certain things and backward for her age, but she's not what you say. A young girl who has held the attention of Monsieur Lachaille is not a little chit.'

A furious shrug of the shoulders set Alicia's black lace quivering.

'All right, all right! With all due respect, then, how did you handle your precious princess?'

'I talked sense to her. I spoke to her of the family. I tried to make her understand that we sink or swim together. I enumerated all the things she could do for herself and for us.'

'And what about nonsense? Did you talk nonsense to her? Didn't you talk to her of love, travel, moonlight, Italy? You must know how to harp on every string. Didn't you tell her that on the other side of the world the sea is phosphorescent, that there are humming-birds in all the flowers, and that you make love under gardenias in full bloom beside a moonlit fountain?'

Madame Alvarez looked at her spirited elder sister with sadness in her eyes.

'I couldn't tell her all that, Alicia, because I know nothing about it. I've never been farther afield than Cobourg and Monte Carlo.'

'Aren't you capable of inventing it?'

'No, Alicia.'

Both fell silent. Alicia, with a gesture, made up her mind.

'Call the chit in to me. We shall see.'

54   When Gilberte came in, Aunt Alicia had resumed all the airs

and graces of a frivolous old lady and was smelling the tea-rose pinned near her chin.

'Good afternoon, my little Gigi.'

'Good afternoon, Aunt Alicia.'

'What is this Inez has been telling me? You have an admirer? And what an admirer! For your first attempt, it's a master-stroke!'

Gilberte acquiesced with a guarded, resigned little smile. She offered to Alicia's darting curiosity a fresh young face, to which the violet-blue shadow in her eyelids and the high colour of her mouth gave an almost artificial effect. For coolness' sake, she had dragged back the hair off her temples with the help of two combs, and this had drawn up the corners of her eyes.

'And it seems you have been playing the naughty girl, and tried your claws on Monsieur Lachaille! Bravo, my brave little girl!'

Gilberte raised incredulous eyes to her aunt.

'Yes, indeed! Bravo! It will only make him all the happier when you are nice to him again.'

'But I am nice to him, Aunt. Only, I don't want to, that's all.'

'Yes, yes, we know. You've sent him packing to his sugar refinery; that's perfect. But don't send him to the Devil; he's quite capable of going. The fact is, you don't love him.'

Gilberte gave a little childish shrug.

'Yes, Aunt, I'm very fond of him.'

'Just what I said, you don't love him. Mind you, there's no harm in that, it leaves you free to act as you please. Ah, if you'd been head over heels in love with him, then I should have been a little anxious. Lachaille is a fine figure of a man. Well built— you've only to look at the photographs of him taken at Deauville in bathing costume. He's famous for that. Yes, I should feel 55 sorry for you, my poor Gigi. To start by having a passionate love-affair—to go away all by your two selves to the other side of the world, forgetting everything in the arms of the man who adores you, listening to the song of love in an eternal spring—surely things of that sort must touch your heart! What does all that say to you?'

'It says to me that when eternal spring is over Monsieur Lachaille will go off with another lady. Or else that the lady—me if you like—will leave Monsieur Lachaille, and Monsieur Lachaille will hurry off to blab the whole story. And then the lady, still me if you like, will have nothing else to do but get into another gentlemen's bed. I don't want that. I'm not changeable by nature, indeed I'm not.'

She crossed her arms over her breasts and shivered slightly.

'Grandmamma, may I have a *cachet Faivre?* I want to go to bed. I feel cold.'

'You great goose!' burst out Aunt Alicia, 'a tuppenny-ha'penny milliner's shop is all you deserve! Be off! Go and marry a bank clerk!'

'If you wish it, Aunt. But I want to go to bed.'

Madame Alvarez put her hand on Gigi's forehead.

'Don't you feel well?'

'I'm all right, Grandmamma. Only I'm sad.'

She leaned her head on Madame Alvarez' shoulder, and, for the first time in her life, closed her eyes pathetically like a grown woman. The two sisters exchanged glances.

'You must know, my Gigi,' said Madame Alvarez, 'that we won't torment you to that extent. If you say you really don't want to—'

'A failure is a failure,' said Alicia caustically. 'We can't go on 56 discussing it for ever.'

'You'll never be able to say you didn't have good advice, and the very best at that,' said Madame Alvarez.

'I know, Grandmamma, but I'm sad, all the same.'

'Why?'

A tear trickled over Gilberte's downy cheek without wetting it, but she did not answer. A brisk peel of the door bell made her jump where she stood.

'Oh, it must be him,' she said. 'it is him! Grandmamma, I don't want to see him! Hide me, Grandmamma!'

At the low, passionate tone of her voice, Aunt Alicia raised an attentive head, and pricked an expert ear. Then she ran to open the door and came back a moment later. Gaston Lachaille, haggard, his eyes bloodshot, followed close behind her.

'Good afternoon, Mamita. Good afternoon, Gigi!' he said airily. 'Please don't move, I've come to retrieve my straw hat.'

None of the three women replied, and his assurance left him.

'Well you might at least say a word to me, even if it's only How-d'you-do?'

Gilberte took a step towards him.

'No,' she said. 'You've not come to retrieve your straw hat. You have another one in your hand. And you would never bother about a hat. You've come to make me more miserable than ever.'

'Really!' burst out Madame Alvarez. 'This is more than I can stomach. How can you Gigi! Here is a man who, out of the goodness of his generous heart—'

'If you please, Grandmamma, just a moment, and I shall have finished.'

Instinctively she straightened her dress, adjusted the buckle of her sash, and marched up to Gaston.

'I've been thinking, Gaston. In fact, I've been thinking a great deal—'

He interrupted her, to stop her saying what he was afraid to hear.

'I swear to you, my darling—'

'No, don't swear to me. I've been thinking I would rather be miserable with you than without you. So . . .'

She tired twice to go on.

'So . . . There you are. How d'you do, Gaston, how d'you do?'

She offered him her cheek, in her usual way. He held her, a little longer than usual, until he felt her relax, and become calm and gentle in his arms. Madame Alvarez seemed about to hurry forward, but Alicia's impatient little hand restrained her.

'Leave well alone. Don't meddle any more. Can't you see she is far beyond us?'

She pointed to Gigi, who was resting a trusting head and the rich abundance of her hair on Lachaille's shoulder.

The happy man turned to Madame Alvarez.

'Mamita,' he said, 'will you do me the honour, the favour, give me the infinite joy of bestowing on me the hand . . .'